JOURNEY TO THE GATES OF HEAVEN

By

Simran Pal

ISBN: 978-93-343-7628-9

Cover Design: Simran Pal

Published by Simran Pal

For more information, visit: [Instagram @simranpal.907]

Email: Simranpal907@gmail.com

Printed in India.

Preface

Before this story began, I often wondered what lay beyond the known — beyond maps, beyond myth, beyond the stories we've always been told.

Journey to the Gates of Heaven was born from that question — a question buried in dusty temples, ancient echoes, and the fire that flickers in those who seek something greater than destiny.

In this novel, you will follow three unlikely companions — Agni, Hansika, and Surya. As they trace the forgotten path once walked by the Pandavas. What they find along the way is not just a route to heaven, but the truth of who they are, and what it means to be worthy.

This story weaves together mythology, fantasy, and humanity. It is a tribute to inner fire, unspoken courage, and the echoes of legends that refuse to fade.

I invite you to take this journey — not just through sacred mountains and cursed forests, but through the spaces within us that ache to be remembered.

— *Simran Pal*

DISCLAIMER

This is a work of fiction. Names, characters, places, and events are the product of the author's imagination or are used fictitiously. Any resemblance to actual events, locales, or persons, living or dead, is purely coincidental.

While inspired by elements of Indian mythology, this story is a fictional reinterpretation and does not claim historical or religious accuracy. The author respects all cultural and religious sentiments and intends only to entertain and inspire through this imaginative journey.

"Some paths don't lead us forward—they lead us inward.

And in walking them, we don't find destinations…

we find who we were always meant to be."

Table of Contents

स्वर्गदुस्तरस्य यात्रा

नायं पन्थां विरुदः धर्मस्य,
यः केवलं स्वार्थंत प्रति नयति।
सत्य, तपः, कुरुणा च मार्गः,
स्वर्गस्य द्वारं प्रबोधितम् ॥

Nāyam panthā virudaḥ dharmasya, yah kevalām svārthām prati nayati. Satyam, tapaḥ, karuṇā ca mārgaḥ, svragasya dvārām prabodhitam.

This is not the path of Dharma, which leads only to selfish desire. Truth, sacrifice, and compassion awaken the true gates of heaven.

Prologue: Whispers of Heaven

Long ago, when war-dust still clung to the bones of kings, and the echoes of the Mahabharata whispered through the folds of mountain winds, five warriors walked their final path.

Barefoot and silent, the Pandavas ascended toward Mount Sumeru—the mythic Gates of Heaven—led not by glory, but by Dharma himself. Behind them lay a world they had ruled, cherished, and lost—its empires turned to ash, its triumphs forgotten by time.

One by one, they fell.

Not to sword, nor curse, nor time—

But to the unseen trials of the soul:

Pride. Partiality. Vanity. Greed. Doubt.

Only Yudhishthira, eldest and weary, reached the gates—stripped of all but truth.

His was not a journey of distance,

But of surrender.

The world forgot that path.

But the mountains remember.

The rivers still murmur its name.

And the stones hold their silence like breath.

And one boy listened.

Agni—a child without lineage, raised by temple fires and the quiet ache of unanswered prayers—found the scroll buried beneath a crumbled altar, hidden under centuries of moss and dust.

Not a myth.

Not a story.

A map.

Etched in ancient script that shimmered with heat, it spoke of an ancient pilgrimage, carved in divine flame. A path once sealed by gods.

Now, awakened again.

But Agni does not seek glory.

He seeks answers—

To the fire that stirs in his blood,

To the faces he's never seen—his parents,

To the question that haunts his silence:

What lies beyond a world that shatters us?

With him walks Hansika—slender and storm-eyed, wrapped in saffron scarf and secrets. She is as sharp as moonlight and twice as quiet. Her gaze sees what others miss, and her loyalty runs deeper than her courage will ever admit.

And Surya, broad-shouldered and rough-palmed, whose cobbler's hammer once echoed through village lanes. A craftsman by trade, but a dreamer at heart—haunted by the ache of being overlooked.

They do not know what awaits them.

They cannot yet see how each step will strip away pride, pain, and illusion—

Until only truth remains.

The road has opened again.

And the gates are waiting.

***

Chapter One:
The Call to Adventure

The sun hung low over the village near Prayag, gilding the cracked mud walls and mango trees in a molten hush. Smoke from morning fires curled into the air, carrying the scent of sandalwood, lentils, and cow dung. Far in the distance, the Ganga shimmered like a silver serpent, whispering stories of gods, of empires long turned to ash, and of wars no one remembered—but the land still did.

The village pulsed with routine—temple bells, chanting priests, the rustle of saris, the clatter of bangles. But for one boy, it was never enough.

Agni, twenty-four, stood alone beneath the gnarled banyan tree that marked the edge of the world he knew. Tall and athletic, with skin like sun-warmed copper and coal-black curls that never quite obeyed, he looked like a myth cast in flesh. His sharp jaw was clean-shaven, his eyes deep brown and burning—always burning—with something unnamed. Not anger. Not wonder. But *fire.* A fire that made elders murmur and children stare.

He wore a sun-faded dhoti, hastily knotted at the waist, and a homespun scarf slung across his shoulder, its ends frayed from too many temple climbs and wind-swept hikes. A leather satchel, heavy with scrolls and secrets, thudded gently against his hip.

To the villagers, he was an oddity.

To the priests, a mystery.

To himself, a question.

He traced a faded Sanskrit verse etched into an ancient stone near the tree's roots—words almost erased by time, but not by him. His fingertips were black with charcoal, his notebook half-filled with codes, maps, and fragments no one else understood.

He had searched temples in Kashi, begged for meaning from silent sadhus in Chitrakoot, and stood barefoot in mossy shrines where no offerings remained. For years, the silence mocked him.

And then—he found it.

Buried beneath a ruined altar, deep in a forgotten shrine, wrapped in silk that smelled of camphor and dust. A scroll. Inked in celestial gold, sealed in silence. The moment he touched it, the wind had stilled. And from the shadows, a figure emerged.

The Older Man—wrapped in layered robes that moved like smoke, his face veiled by time. Unmoving. Watching.

Agni had clutched the scroll and fled.

Since that day, the scroll had not left his hut, hidden beneath a loose tile on the floor. He had read it nightly. Studied it until his eyes burned.

It was not a myth.

Not a riddle.

It was a map.

A trail carved not by kings, but by gods. The forgotten final journey of the Pandavas. It spoke of places never marked on any map, and of Mount Sumeru, the mountain where the mortal and divine blurred.

Tonight, he would leave. Alone.

Not even Hansika knew.

Especially not Hansika.

She was his sun and shadow. A girl of twenty-one with hazel eyes sharp as flint, skin kissed by early monsoons, and long black hair she never seemed to care for but always looked perfect. She wore travel-tucked kurtas and a scarf that smelled of salt and rose. She laughed too easily. Argued like she was born for war. And always—*always*—found him.

She had a way of looking at him that made Agni feel both seen and buried. She mocked his silences, but never stopped walking beside them.

He hadn't told her because he knew she would follow.

Because she always did.

And this… this was a fire he had to walk through alone.

That evening, Agni sat cross-legged inside his hut. The walls flickered with lam plight, casting the room in gold and shadow. Scrolls and palm-leaf manuscripts were stacked against one side, a constellation chart pinned beside a dried marigold garland. The air smelled of turmeric, ink, and something older—hope.

He unrolled the scroll again. The symbols shimmered.

"*Beyond the place where rivers meet and gods bathe,*

A silent path opens under moonless skies.

Follow not roads of men, but echoes of virtue.

The mountain of truth rises where the self dissolves."

These were not just verses. They were trials.

He marked his map again:

- Hidden shrine near **Chitrakoot**
- The **Ghaghara Forest**, said to echo even dreams
- The **Vindhya Caves**, untouched by light
- And finally… **Mount Sumeru**

He closed his eyes.

Then came the knock.

Sharp. Intentional.

He blew out the lamp.

The knock again.

Agni opened the door—and there she was.

Hansika. Framed by twilight. Eyes bright with questions.

"You haven't come to the river in three days," she said, stepping inside without waiting.

"I've been busy."

"With what? Skulking around temples? Digging through graves?"

He smiled. "You're dramatic."

"You're hiding something."

Her voice was soft—but sharp. He loved that about her. Feared it too.

"If something's wrong, Agni, tell me."

He wanted to. Desperately.

But he didn't.

"I'm just... figuring something out."

She stared. Then left.

And he let her.

By morning, the village was awake with bells and blacksmiths. Surya, twenty-three, hunched in his father's old workshop, hammering a sandal heel into shape. Slender, but strong, with broad shoulders, tall and handsome with soot-lined arms. His pants were torn at the cuffs, his scarf too worn—but his work was perfect.

He kept glancing at the forest's edge, where whispers traveled faster than light.

Later, by the river, he found Hansika staring into the current.

"You look like you're about to burn something down," he said.

She didn't smile. "He's leaving."

Surya's chest tightened. "Agni?"

She nodded.

"He's hiding something big. And I'm going to find out what."

Surya looked away.

She didn't see him the way she saw Agni.

And yet… he would still follow.

He always did.

"Tonight?" he asked.

Her silence was the only answer he needed.

***

Chapter Two:
Whispers of the Unknown

Night draped the village like a veil woven from prayers and silence. The breeze carried the scent of damp earth and burnt ghee from the evening aarti. Somewhere, a cow lowed. Somewhere else, the Ganga murmured like a mother singing her child to sleep.

But Agni was wide awake.

He moved through the village shadows with practiced stealth, a loosely wrapped shawl trailing behind him like smoke. Beneath it, his dhoti was tightly tucked for travel. His lean, athletic form moved with quiet purpose—years of climbing ruins and sneaking into ancient temples had taught him how to vanish in plain sight.

His satchel thumped gently against his side, heavy with the weight of belief.

Inside it:

- The sealed scroll, wax pressed with the mark of fire
- A clay vial of sacred ash
- Parchment maps sketched from temple walls
- The bead from the flame trial—warm even now

He passed the old stone arch at the village boundary. Beyond it, the path faded into the dense forest, where no one wandered after sunset.

No one but Agni.

He reached the base of a hill and crouched in the clearing, lit faintly by moonlight.

Before him: the Shrine of the Forgotten Flame, half-swallowed by roots and time. The cracked altar bore a nearly faded carving—a flame inside a rising sun.

Agni placed his palm on the stone.

Nothing.

He whispered a verse from the scroll.

Then, carefully, he laid the scroll on the altar.

The moment the red wax seal touched the carving, the stone pulsed.

A faint glow—like embered breath—stirred from beneath the ancient mark.

Behind a nearby neem tree, Hansika exhaled sharply.

She had followed him through brambles and shadows, clutching her scarf tightly. Her red salwar and travel-worn kurti were muddied, but her steps were careful. Her long black braid had come partially undone, and sweat clung to her brow—but her eyes, hazel and sharp, didn't waver.

She had seen Agni sneak out before. But tonight was different.

She stepped forward to get a better view—

Snap.

A dry twig betrayed her.

Agni's fire sparked instantly, torch flaring in his hand.

"Who's there?!"

She stepped into the light. "It's me."

Agni stared, disbelief cutting through the firelight. "Hansika?! What are you doing here?"

"I could ask you the same," she shot back, brushing a leaf from her shoulder.

"You shouldn't be here."

"Clearly, neither should you."

They stared at each other—silhouetted by the flickering altar flame. A thousand words hovered between them.

Hansika folded her arms. "So. This is it. The secret?"

Agni didn't answer.

She stepped closer to the altar, eyeing the scroll.

"This is what's been keeping you up at night? Ancient riddles and glowing rocks?"

"It's real," he said, voice low. "It's all real. The path Pandavas took to reach the Heavens!"

Hansika let out a breath—half laugh, half frustration. "Agni, come on. I know you believe in… things. Sacred geometry, secret paths, divine echoes—but this? The Pandavas' ascent?"

He said nothing.

"You honestly think heaven left a map behind? For you to find?"

"It's not a map," Agni whispered. "It's a call."

"A call to what? Madness?"

His jaw tensed. "To truth."

Hansika looked around at the shrine, then back to him. "Agni… I know you're searching. For your parents. For your fire. For something to make sense. But this isn't the way. These stories were meant to guide us spiritually—not literally."

His voice was quieter now. "What if they were both?"

She shook her head. "You're chasing shadows."

"I've seen signs. Carvings. Alignments. This scroll appeared to me the night of Kartik Purnima. The Older Man—he was there. He's been watching me since Kashi."

Hansika took a deep breath. "You're tired. Obsessed. You want this so badly, you're making it real."

His expression didn't change. "Because it is."

She looked at him—really looked at him.

This wasn't some childish dream. His eyes burned with purpose. Conviction.

And that terrified her.

The flame at the altar shimmered brighter between them, as if listening.

Hansika reached out, touching his arm. "You don't have to do this. We can go back. Tomorrow. I'll help you research. We'll ask the priest at Ramghat—"

"I'm leaving," he interrupted.

She froze.

He turned to face her fully. "Tonight."

Hansika blinked. "Alone?"

He paused.

The silence stretched.

Finally, she whispered, "I can't let you go."

"You don't believe."

"No. I don't," she admitted. "But I believe in you. And someone has to keep you from burning yourself alive chasing the sky."

Agni looked at her—and for a moment, the weight of his solitude lifted.

"...Alright," he said quietly. "But I won't slow down."

Hansika's smile was faint. "I never asked you to."

Suddenly, a growl echoed from the tree line.

They turned.

A black dog stood watching them—unnaturally still, eyes glowing green.

Agni tensed.

Hansika whispered, "What in the gods' names..."

"They say Dharma walks the earth in the form of a dog," Agni murmured.

The creature blinked—once.

Then it turned and vanished into the woods.

A tremor passed beneath their feet.

The flame at the altar ignited, rising high before settling into a steady, golden glow.

The shrine pulsed.

And the forest sighed.

The path had accepted them.

Even if she didn't believe in it… yet.

Elsewhere...

High beyond the mortal plane, among clouds blackened by forgotten oaths, Raktadeva stirred.

Ash fell from his armor like dead stars.

He looked east—toward Agni.

"They awaken the scroll," he muttered. "And seek the path."

A grin like a split wound spread across his face.

"Let them walk it."

Back in the Village...

Surya stood in the doorway of his workshop, the moonlight painting silver on his bare arms.

He had seen Hansika slip away.

Had seen the look in her eyes.

It wasn't love.

It was worry.

And it was always for Agni.

Surya looked down at his calloused hands.

Tomorrow, he would follow them.

Not because he believed in gates or gods.

But because he believed in her.

***

Chapter Three:
Silent Preparations

The days that followed blurred into a rhythm of secrecy—whispers traded like currency, glances that spoke louder than words, and footsteps swallowed by the dust of narrow village paths.

Before the roosters crowed and the fires were lit, Agni and Hansika met in the shadow of the old banyan tree, its roots coiled like sleeping serpents. The dew-drenched earth cooled their feet as they moved in silence through mango groves, where unripe fruit dangled like questions yet unspoken. They passed shrines with cracked bells and abandoned fields that still remembered war, moving like conspirators in a story only they knew.

Agni's eyes—deep brown, always intense—rarely blinked now. A thin stubble had begun to shadow his clean-shaven jaw. The fire in his palm had not flared in days, but it hadn't left. It lived under his skin now.

Hansika walked beside him, her red kurti dusted with travel, a scarf wound around her shoulders with practiced care. Her hazel eyes—sharp, searching—glanced sideways at him as they knelt beside a stream that gleamed silver under the soft sun.

She filled a copper flask, watching the surface ripple. "Do you really think this will lead to heaven?" she asked, her tone light, but her question real.

Agni didn't answer immediately. He was running his thumb along the scroll's edge, now warm to the touch—as if the script pulsed with breath.

"I don't know if it's heaven," he said at last. "But I know it leads somewhere the world forgot."

Hansika scoffed softly. "So… still convinced a bunch of old verses are guiding you to paradise?"

He looked at her, eyes calm. "I'm not chasing paradise. I'm chasing a truth that survived the silence."

She didn't reply. But her brows creased.

Somewhere behind them, a woodpecker knocked on a dying sal tree.

But they weren't the only ones carrying secrets.

Surya had noticed.

He noticed the shift in their patterns. Agni, once always wandering the temple corridors asking impossible questions, now walked with purpose but avoided crowds. Hansika, once full of quips and chaos, now vanished at dawn, her return marked only by mud-streaked salwars and unusually guarded silences.

It wasn't just detachment.

It was departure.

And Surya, for all his jokes and easy charm, wasn't blind.

That evening, from behind the storage shed near the blacksmith's courtyard, he watched Hansika slipping a bundle of food—wrapped in linen and tied with red string—into Agni's satchel. Her fingers lingered there a moment too long.

Surya's jaw clenched.

In his workshop that night, Surya stitched in silence.

The walls were blackened from years of fire, the air thick with leather and smoke. He sat cross-legged on the earthen floor, oil lamp flickering near his tools. His hands were steady—rough-palmed, callused, knuckles scarred from years of work. But tonight, even his best craftsmanship couldn't ease the weight inside his chest.

His grandmother, blind in one eye but sharp in spirit, called from the veranda, "Your hands are steady, boy… but your thoughts? Wild as monsoon clouds."

He chuckled without mirth. "Some clouds need thunder before they rain."

She only hummed.

Later that night, Surya stepped out under the darkening sky, scarf tossed loosely over his shoulder, hammer tucked into his waistband like an afterthought. The moon was sharp and bright—watching everything.

He walked without sound, barefoot through neem groves, his steps sure but silent. And there—just beyond the bend—he saw them.

Agni and Hansika.

Crouched beside a shrine stone, firelight playing over their features. Agni's brows furrowed, his athletic frame hunched over a scroll. Hansika leaned beside him, arms folded, her braid catching light like a river at dusk.

They didn't look like villagers.

They looked like people who no longer belonged here.

"Pilgrims," Surya muttered.

Then, quieter:

"Or fugitives."

He watched until the torch dimmed.

Then slipped back into the night.

The next evening, as the sun sank low behind the sacred hill, the village settled into its twilight rituals—bells chimed, women sang lullabies, smoke curled from brass pots.

Surya sat on his veranda, stitching a thick-heeled sandal. Each knot was deliberate. Each pierce of the needle whispered an old truth: You walk best when you walk for yourself.

But today, he felt like he was being left behind.

Agni—burning, unreadable, chasing legends.

Hansika—storm-eyed and loyal to a cause she didn't even believe in.
And him?
He was just the ground beneath them.
He had always been.

That night, near the old well where wishes died and secrets gathered, Surya saw them again.
Agni knelt, inspecting the stone circle. Hansika stood above him like a sentinel, her eyes sharp, scarf rippling slightly with the wind.

Surya approached, casual but direct. "You two look like you've been summoned by the gods themselves. Something sacred in that moss?"
Agni startled. Hansika tensed.
"Nothing important," Agni said. "Just... stones."
"Strange," Surya replied, "how nervous old stones make people lately."
They didn't laugh.

He dropped the teasing. "I've known you both since we scraped knees in temple courtyards. If you're in danger—tell me."

Hansika looked at Agni.

The glance was brief, but it said everything.

Agni rose, brushing his hands. "We're figuring things out."

"Not much of an answer."

"No," Agni said, "it's not."

The silence between them felt ancient. Like it had waited through centuries to speak.

A bell rang in the distance.

Surya's voice dropped. "Secrets have a price. Sometimes a heavy one."

He turned and left—his shadow longer than his doubts.

Elsewhere…

Far from temples and trees, beyond the known edges of scripture, Raktadeva stirred.

He sat upon a throne of scorched bone, obsidian chains curled at his feet. The scroll's echo—its ancient resonance—had reached even him.

He rose.

Each movement scattered dust from ages lost.

"They seek the flame," he rasped. "Fools."

His voice was like sand over glass. A ruin given breath.

"They think fire will give them truth."

He raised his hand.

A spark danced on his fingertip—black, cold, alive.

"Let them learn how easily it consumes."

And with that…

He stepped into the shadows.

***

Chapter Four:
The Secret Path

The forest behind Prayagpur was older than memory. It did not simply grow—it waited. Roots gnarled like the fingers of forgotten saints twisted through the earth, while branches tangled above like a net spun by time. The canopy shrouded the sun, leaving the ground in a half-light that flickered like dreams on the edge of sleep.

Agni stepped between the roots with reverence, his movements quiet but certain. He carried only what mattered: the scroll, the obsidian-flint lamp, sacred ash in a clay vial, and belief—burning, bright, unwavering. His clothes were humble: a cotton tunic, a coarse shawl wrapped across his chest, and simple leather sandals. But there was something regal about him tonight, something unspoken. He walked like someone chosen by forces older than gods.

Beside him moved Hansika, her frame cloaked in a deep red kurti and cotton salwar, scarf pulled tight around her shoulders. She was light on her feet, yet every step carried weight. The forest didn't frighten her. But the boy ahead did—because he was walking into myth like it was memory.

The path was barely visible, overtaken by creepers and years of silence. Lantern light wavered over moss-covered stones, fallen idols, and the skeletal remains of temples swallowed by root and soil.

After nearly an hour of walking in wordless focus, Agni stopped near a towering banyan whose roots had enveloped a collapsed altar. Its bark was cracked and weeping resin. At its base, a flat stone bore a symbol: a spiral flame inside a circle. Faded but unmistakable.

Agni crouched beside it. His fingers brushed away dust like it was sacred.

"This is it," he whispered. "The first marker."

Hansika crouched beside him, brow furrowed. "How did you know this would be here?"

"I didn't," he said softly. "But the carvings in Ujjain spoke of a banyan altar west of the confluence. The scroll hinted at a hidden passage from a 'place where shadow drinks flame.' This is it."

Hansika touched the carving. It felt warm. She glanced at Agni—at the way his eyes studied every detail like scripture, like memory.

"You've been chasing this for a long time, haven't you?"

Agni didn't reply. But his silence said yes.

They built a small camp under the banyan's hanging roots. As Hansika rolled out a mat and checked their food supply—dried rice cakes, lentil flour, smoked tamarind—Agni spread the scroll between two flat stones. Its script shimmered faintly in the firelight, as if acknowledging the altar.

Hansika peered at it again, arms folded tightly. "And you still believe this path leads to Mount Sumeru? To the Gates of Heaven?"

Agni didn't answer immediately. Instead, he traced a line of ancient ink.

"I don't know if heaven waits at the end," he said finally. "But something does. Something the world forgot."

Hansika sighed. "Agni… just listen to how that sounds. You're talking about a story from scripture. A divine path. A climb that only Yudhishthira completed. You think that's real?"

"I don't think," Agni said, voice firm. "I know."

She looked away. "You're chasing a myth."

"And what if the myth is true?" he asked, leaning toward her. "What if we've stopped believing only because no one bothered to look?"

Hansika stared at him. Firelight danced in his eyes, and for a moment, she saw not just a seeker—but a boy who had stared into empty skies for answers that never came.

"People die for less than what you're doing," she whispered.

"I'd rather die searching," he replied, "than live with questions that burn through my sleep."

She didn't argue again that night.

Elsewhere in the village…

Surya's hammer struck the wooden block with a dull thud.

He hadn't worked a sandal in two days.

He told his grandmother he was sick. He wasn't.

He was watching.

From the shadows beyond the mango grove, he had seen Hansika and Agni slip into the forest with ropes, cloth bundles, and something folded reverently beneath Agni's tunic. He didn't need a scroll to know what that meant.

And it burned.

Not because they were leaving.

But because they hadn't asked him.

Surya stared at the unfinished sandal in his lap. It was well-shaped, sturdy. But it looked wrong somehow. Pointless. Like a foot without a path.

"I built the world's best shoes," he muttered bitterly, "and they still walk without me."

Later that night…

The forest was cooler now. Owls blinked from the trees. Insects buzzed like prayers between the leaves.

Agni and Hansika stood near an old well, wrapping their belongings in cloth. Hansika tucked the scroll into a brass cylinder and tied it to Agni's belt.

"You're sure about this?" she asked.

Agni nodded. "The Ghaghara Forest is next. From there, the trail moves west."

Hansika hesitated. "And if the path vanishes?"

"Then we make our own."

A voice cut through the trees behind them.

"That's the stupidest thing I've ever heard."

They both turned.

Surya stood just beyond the clearing, arms folded, breath ragged. He wore rugged pants, a faded scarf, and a satchel slung across one shoulder. His boots were new. His eyes were not.

"You think the Pandavas left trail markers for barefoot children to follow?" he said coldly.

Agni straightened. "Surya—"

Hansika took a step forward. "He's not trying to find heaven—"

"Then what?" Surya barked. "Answers? Purpose? You think you'll find it in a cave somewhere, Agni? While the rest of us sit in our huts and stitch leather to survive?"

Agni was silent.

Surya turned to Hansika. "And you? You believe in this?"

Hansika opened her mouth—then stopped.

"No," she said honestly. "I don't."

Surya's eyebrows rose.

"But I believe in him," she added quietly. "And I'm going to make sure he doesn't lose himself chasing the sky."

The silence that followed was thick.

Finally, Surya looked down.

"You two are idiots."

Agni smirked. "That's fair."

Surya exhaled through his nose, then flung his satchel to the ground.

"Fine. I'm coming."

Hansika blinked. "What?"

"You'll get lost without me," Surya said. "Agni will forget to eat. You'll try to climb the Vindhyas barefoot. Someone needs to remind you to sleep and not die."

Agni shook his head. "We didn't ask you to—"

"No," Surya snapped. "But you should've."

He paused, eyes sharp.

"I don't believe in gods. But I believe in keeping people alive. So don't make me regret it."

Agni stepped forward and extended his hand.

Surya stared at it.

Then took it.

"Welcome to the stupidest quest in history," Agni said.

"Feels about right," Surya replied.

Three figures stepped deeper into the trees.

The scroll pulsed against Agni's side.

The wind shifted.

And the forest opened its mouth.

Not in warning—

But in welcome.

The journey had truly begun.

***

Chapter Five:

Into the Wild

The wind whispered through the sal trees as Agni, Hansika, and Surya stood at the forest's edge. Behind them, Prayagpur still slumbered under the gauze of early dawn—its temple bells silent, its rooftops still bathed in the gold hush of morning mist. They stood at the edge not just of forest, but of the known world.

Agni stepped forward first.

He wore a dark dhoti and cotton scarf wrapped diagonally across his chest. His obsidian blade was sheathed at his back, hidden beneath folds of fabric. Beneath his tunic, the scroll pressed against his chest, radiating a low heat—like a second heartbeat. His eyes, brown and burning with resolve, scanned the trail ahead.

Beside him, Hansika adjusted the strap of her satchel. Dressed in a travel-ready red kurti and cream salwar, her hair was tied in a thick braid. Her scarf was pinned across her shoulder, weighted down by tiny iron prayer charms. She had packed like a healer: vials of neem oil, bandages, dried berries, firestones. She didn't speak—but her silence was focused, not fearful. Every step she took was deliberate. She had chosen this.

Trailing behind them, Surya muttered something under his breath. His rough pants were dusted at the cuffs, and a leather satchel slapped lightly against his side. His cobbler's hammer, once used to mend soles, now hung at his waist like a symbol of defiance.

"You never know when you'll need to fix a sandal," he had said that morning, "or knock some sense into someone."

No one had laughed.

They stepped into the wild—and the forest swallowed them whole.

Before the Departure

Just hours earlier, as the village prepared for dawn, Surya's grandmother stood by the fire pit outside their home.

"Where are you off to at this hour?" she asked, squinting suspiciously as he packed his bag with more than just shoemaker's tools.

"An order," Surya lied smoothly, not meeting her gaze. "A zamindar in Kashi needs special work. Could take a week."

She grunted. "If you don't return with coin, don't return at all."

"I'll return with more than coin," he muttered.

She didn't hear him.

Meanwhile, Hansika had stood at the edge of her home's tulsi courtyard, tying her braid tightly, her satchel hidden beneath her shawl.

Her mother, sweeping the threshold, paused. "Leaving early again? You haven't even eaten."

Hansika smiled tightly. "There's a women's herbal gathering in the forest village near Ghaghara. I'll be back in a few days."

Her mother frowned. "Alone?"

"Kalindi's sister will meet me on the way."

That was the lie that stuck.

Her mother didn't argue further. Just handed her a packet of turmeric and said, "Offer this at the shrine if you pass one."

Hansika nodded, pressed her forehead to her mother's shoulder—and walked away.

In the Forest

By midday, light had all but vanished beneath the thick canopy of leaves. The forest breathed in shades of green and shadow, damp earth rising like memory from the floor.

They paused beside a mossy stream, where sunlight struck water like scattered coins.

"This doesn't look like any merchant path," Surya muttered, eyeing the unfamiliar terrain.

Agni crouched near the stream. "It isn't. We're not walking toward a city. We're walking toward a forgotten verse."

Hansika pulled out a worn, hand-sketched map, its paper layered with markings from the scroll—symbols translated through riddle and gut instinct.

"There," she pointed. "The banyan."

And they saw it.

A massive tree, split clean down the middle. Its roots curved like claws, its arch forming a green doorway draped in vines and wildflowers.

Even the birds fell silent.

They stepped through.

The forest changed.

No more rustling. No chirping. Even their own breathing sounded distant.

Agni led them through the thickets, eyes scanning every tree trunk and stone. Symbols emerged—tiny carvings of fire, a mace, a crown. Stories long buried in bark.

Then a fallen idol, half-buried in moss. Bhima, frozen mid-strike, his mace shattered.

Surya touched the stone. "You really think they passed through here?"

Agni nodded slowly. "I think the land remembers them. And now it's watching us."

That Night

They camped beneath a crooked neem tree, its branches like gnarled arms cradling the stars. A small fire crackled between them. Hansika brewed tea in a brass cup. Agni pored over the scroll. Surya sharpened his hammer's edge with a whetstone, more out of nervous energy than need.

Suddenly—a rustle.

Surya rose to his feet.

From the trees emerged a fox, its coat streaked with ash, its eyes glowing faint green. It didn't snarl. It didn't blink. It just… watched.

Then, without sound, it turned and disappeared into the dark.

"A spirit," Hansika whispered.

"No," Agni said. "A guide."

—

That night, Agni dreamed of fire.

Not burning—but living.

The Older Man appeared once more. Made of flame, but calm as dusk.

"You cannot walk forward without leaving something behind. The fire you carry consumes more than your fears. It consumes memory. Be careful what you offer it."

Agni awoke gasping.

The fire still burned.

Untouched.

Hansika stirred beside him. "It should have gone out by now."

He nodded. "I think the fox… left us something."

He pointed.

Tiny scorch marks like glowing ember footprints led away from the camp.

They followed them through the hush of dawn, pushing past vines and mossy boulders, until the trail ended at the base of a staircase—half-buried in dirt and bone.

Above: a shrine.

Cracked, crumbling, and covered in ivy.

"This," Agni whispered, "is a remnant."

Carvings of ancient warriors lined the doorway. The flame-and-scale sigil of Dharma pulsed faintly on the lintel.

Then—a gust.

A figure appeared.

Barefoot. Hooded. Cloaked in dust. Holding a bronze staff carved with mantras.

"I am Vritaka," the figure said. "Keeper of Memory. You walk upon sacred ground. Before you pass—offer truth."

He struck the ground.

And the world fractured.

The Trial of Shared Truth

The world twisted—into a mirrored hall.

But the mirrors didn't reflect them.

They reflected their wounds.

Agni saw his younger self, reaching toward a burning temple.

"You seek your parents," the child whispered.

"But is it truth… or ego? You want to be chosen."

"I want peace," Agni whispered back. "I want to know why I was left behind."

The mirror melted.

Hansika saw her home. Her mother weeping. Agni walking away.

"You follow him because you want him to turn," said a voice.

"I follow because I choose to. Not because he sees me."

The mirror cracked.

Surya saw a thousand villagers laughing.

"You're no warrior. No prince. You make sandals."

He stepped forward.

"I walked the same stones. That makes me enough."

The mirror vanished.

They awoke back at the shrine.

Vritaka stood at the door.

"You have spoken with honesty. Not perfection. But purpose."

He stepped aside.

Inside lay a golden medallion, etched with the scale and the flame.

Agni picked it up.

Its warmth spread through him like truth.

"This is your token," Vritaka said. "But beware—truth will rise again, and ask more of you."

Then he was gone.

And the shrine crumbled to dust.

They walked on.

No one spoke.

Hansika clutched her satchel tighter.

Surya clenched his jaw.

And Agni… stared at the medallion.

Heaven might lie ahead.

But something darker was already stirring behind them.

***

Chapter Six:
The Forest of Whispers

The valley unfurled before them like a wound—its trees hunched and crooked like ribs pressed through rotting cloth, their bark stained in hues of bruise and blood. Mist slithered between tangled roots like serpents on a hunt. The air was cold—not the bite of nightfall, but the deep, marrow-chilling cold of memory. Something in this forest remembered what even time had tried to forget.

Agni stepped cautiously, his sandals brushing leaf-littered soil. The deeper they ventured, the heavier each breath became—like they weren't just walking through the forest, but into it. The canopy above grew thick and strangling, barely letting through slivers of pale morning light.

"This wasn't on the scroll," Surya muttered. His voice, usually full of sarcasm or steel, now carried unease.

Agni didn't answer immediately. He ran his palm along a twisted trunk marked with spirals that pulsed faintly beneath his touch—almost like veins.

"It wasn't supposed to be here," he said softly.

Hansika reached out to a different tree—this one bore runes she didn't recognize. As her fingers brushed the grooves, the wood pulsed—slow and rhythmic, like a heartbeat. She jerked her hand back.

"Then why," she whispered, "does it feel like it's been waiting for us?"

The trees creaked in response.

And then… the forest whispered.

Not in any known language—but in breath, in pressure, in understanding.

They stepped into a clearing.

And the world twisted.

No walls separated them. No illusions engulfed them. They walked together—but each step grew heavier, as if the ground beneath them remembered every doubt, every lie, every unspoken truth.

Agni's fire flickered at his fingertips.

Hansika's pulse raced in her throat.

Surya's fists clenched around empty air.

They didn't see the roots creeping forward—three thick tendrils sliding across moss. One looped around Agni's ankle. One brushed Hansika's braid. One coiled tightly around Surya's wrist.

They didn't notice.

Until it was too late.

Agni's Trial

Agni stumbled forward into a new clearing—bare earth scorched black, the ground glowing with faint ember-light. Fire bloomed around him—warm, soft, strangely comforting.

In the center stood a cloaked figure, made of ash and smoke.

He stepped forward.

"Fire?" Agni asked, raising his palm. Nothing ignited.

The figure turned—and it was Raktadeva.

But this time, it wasn't a memory.

It wasn't an illusion.

It was him. Watching.

"You burn too brightly," Raktadeva said, his voice smooth and venomous. "And still you see nothing."

Agni backed away—but behind him, fire closed in like a mouth ready to devour.

"You walk to heaven. But you carry ruin."

"I carry hope," Agni said.

"You carry legacy," Raktadeva spat. "You want to be remembered, not reunited."

Agni's face twisted. "That's not true."

Raktadeva's eyes burned. "Then let them fall. Let them burn. Walk alone, if your truth is so strong."

The world snapped.

Hansika and Surya crumbled into ash at Agni's feet.

Agni dropped to his knees, horror carved into his breath.

"No…"

A voice rose in him—not his, but familiar.

Dharma's voice.

"Truth does not ask you to burn others to shine."

Agni drove his fist into the earth.

The fire returned.

Raktadeva vanished into smoke.

But his words lingered like poison.

Hansika's Trial

Crying.

Soft. Familiar. Painful.

Hansika turned and saw her mother—curled in a corner, sobbing.

And behind the tears- herself, younger, watching through a cracked doorway.

Outside that door: Agni.

His back to her.

His voice low as he whispered to someone else.

Hansika called his name.

He didn't turn.

A voice echoed behind her—her own, but older, brittle with cynicism:

"He doesn't see you. You only matter when you bleed for him."

Hansika's fists clenched.

"I followed him because I chose to," she said through gritted teeth.

"No," the voice whispered, circling her like smoke. "You followed because you wanted to be chosen."

"I still want to matter," she said. "But not for him. For me."

She stepped forward—and the memory shattered like glass.

Surya's Trial

Light blinded him.

He stood on a raised platform.

Applause roared like thunder. His name echoed from the skies.

Hansika stood beside him, smiling. Agni bowed beneath the stage.

Surya smiled back.

He turned.

The audience—hundreds of faces—were bleeding from their mouths. Their lips sewn shut with wire.

Their hands clapped.

Not from love.

From obedience.

Above him stood a puppetmaster cloaked in white.

"They cheer because they fear you," it said. "They don't love you. They submit."

Surya's breath trembled. His hammer slipped from his belt.

He tore the crown from his head.

"I don't need to be above them," he said. "I need to walk beside them."

The lights shattered.

They stumbled from the clearing—not screaming, not crying.

Silent.

Not broken.

But changed.

Hansika touched her braid—it had come half undone. She didn't bother fixing it.

Surya looked at his palm—scarred where he'd clutched something in the illusion.

Agni stood quietly. The scroll at his chest pulsed with heat.

"I don't want to talk about what I saw," Surya muttered.

"Neither do I," Agni said.

Hansika reached forward, linking her fingers with theirs.

"But we keep going."

The forest thinned.

And then—the river.

Black as oil, flat as a mirror. It didn't ripple. It didn't breathe.

The sky was reflected in its surface, yet no clouds passed above.

Bones lined the shore.

Old bones.

Some still fresh.

A crooked sign stood, nearly buried in moss.

"To cross is to be known. To survive is to be true."

Agni crouched, whispering, "It's not water. It's memory."

Hansika trembled. "Another trial."

They built a raft—Surya tying reeds and rope. Hansika muttering prayers. Agni blessing the vessel with fire.

They stepped aboard.

Halfway across, a figure appeared on the raft.

Faceless. Hooded. Silent.

He handed each of them a cup filled with inky black liquid.

His voice was the sound of closing doors:

"Truth will ask who you are beneath who you pretend to be."

They drank.

They didn't scream.

But they felt something inside them… peel.

Not illusion.

Not memory.

Truth.

Vaikara

The raft scraped onto stone.

A figure rose on the far bank—obsidian-armored, taller than any man.

His blade glowed like molten glass. His eyes blazed like sorrow turned solid.

"I am Vaikara," he thundered. "Once sentinel to Raktadeva. Now guardian of truth."

Agni stepped forward, fire circling his wrists.

"We didn't come to fight."

"But you will," Vaikara growled. "Only the unshaken pass."

Surya raised his hammer.

Hansika drew both blades.

Vaikara charged.

His blade carved thunder from stone. Sparks flew.

Agni burned sigils into the air, shielding them.

Hansika darted—cutting low and fast. Surya absorbed each blow with grit and blood.

Then—

Hansika screamed: "You're not fighting us—you're fighting yourself!"

Vaikara paused.

Just for a breath.

Agni struck the earth.

A Dharma sigil blazed upward—consuming Vaikara's blade.

He dropped to one knee.

And drew a second sword from his back.

It glowed with silver fire, runes etched across its length:

"Yatra satyam, tatra tejaḥ."

Where there is truth, there is fire.

He handed it to Agni.

"This blade remembers," he said. "As must you."

Agni accepted it.

And the blade breathed.

Vaikara stepped into the river.

And vanished.

They stood in silence.

Hansika looked at Agni like she was seeing him for the first time.

Surya wiped his bloodied hand.

Agni stared at the blade.

Above them, the mist broke.

A single star blinked through the canopy—pointing north.

Mount Sumeru was no longer a myth.

It was waiting.

And so they walked.

***

Chapter Seven:
The Chamber of Echoes

The cursed river faded behind them, its obsidian waters swallowed by tangled roots and windless silence.

Before them rose the cliffs—no gentle slope or forested ridge, but colossal black rock, jagged and fractured, as if some god had driven his blade into the earth and cleaved it open. Cracks ran up the stone like veins. Thunder murmured overhead, though the sky remained dry.

"This doesn't look like a mountain," Surya muttered. "It looks like… a tomb."

Agni ran his fingers along the base of the stone. "Not a tomb," he said. "A vault."

Hansika stepped closer. The cliff face vibrated faintly, and beneath the overgrowth she uncovered a glowing symbol: the spiral flame inside a circle.

"It's the same seal from the scroll," she whispered.

Agni nodded. "This is the next trial. The real one."

He pressed his palm against the glyph.

The cliffs groaned—not like stone cracking, but like doors sighing open. The seal sank into the rock, and with a hiss of cold breath, the wall split apart, revealing a hollow interior lit by no flame, but pulsing with golden luminescence.

The temperature dropped instantly.

They stepped inside.

Behind them, the entrance sealed shut, trapping the warmth—and the world—outside.

The space was not carved. It was grown—as if time itself had worn this chamber into sacred shape.

They stood within a perfect circle; the floor smooth stone etched with ancient mandalas and mantras that shifted faintly underfoot. Four towering archways stood around them, leading into blackness. No doors, just frames.

Above them, glowing script spiraled around the dome's ceiling like a crown:

"सत्य मार्ग दर्शक है।

असत्य मार्ग को चक्रीय बनाता है।

मौन मृत्यु है।"

"Truth shows the path.

Falsehood loops the path.

Silence leads to death."

In the center, a raised circular platform hummed.

As Agni stepped onto it, the room **awakened**.

A tremor shook the walls.

Runes blazed.

Puzzle One:

The platform beneath their feet flared to life. A grid of nine symbols appeared—each square pulsing with faint light and ancient script.

In the air above, the trial's rule glowed in fire:

"नव प्रतीकों में केवल एक असत्य है।

सत्य पर पग रखोगे तो पीछे लौटोगे।

असत्य ही आगे ले जाएगा।"

"Among nine, only one is false.

Step on truth, and be sent back.

Step on the lie—and proceed."

The symbols:

1. A crowned crow
2. A moon with a serpent circling it
3. A river flowing skyward
4. A tree made of bells
5. A sun in chains
6. A man holding a flame over water
7. A bow turned into a lotus
8. A mirror reflecting nothing
9. A chariot pulled by wolves

Hansika furrowed her brow. "Some of these… they're symbolic. Poetic, even."

"But we need logic," Agni said. "Mythic, yes. But grounded."

Surya stepped forward. "The chained sun. Can't happen. You can eclipse a sun, not bind it."

Agni disagreed. "Symbolically, dharma binds all things—even the divine."

Hansika scanned the grid. "The crow. Crows are messengers of death. But a crowned crow? That's a lie."

"Unless the crown is symbolic—messenger of fate," Agni countered.

The wall behind them began to rotate inward—slow, grinding stone ready to crush.

Hansika pointed. "The mirror reflecting nothing. That's a lie. Mirrors show something—even if it's false."

Agni didn't hesitate. He stepped on the mirror square.

The grinding stopped.

A soft chime rang out.

The floor beneath the mirror tile glowed.

The first archway illuminated with amber light.

Puzzle Two:

They stepped into the second chamber—a labyrinth of polished stone and copper, inscribed with slokas from the

Rigveda. Every surface shimmered with reflective gold, and the path split into three.

A voice boomed:

"वास्तविकता पहचानो।

छाया से बचो।

समय सीमित है।"

"Find reality.

Avoid shadow.

Time is limited."

Agni turned—and Hansika was gone.

Surya vanished next.

They had been separated.

Each wandered different tunnels. Every surface echoed their steps. Sometimes, they heard each other's voices—but from wrong directions. Sometimes, their own footsteps repeated when they stopped.

Hansika used an old trick: dipping her fingers into kumkum and dragging a line along the wall. But one wall absorbed it—no color remained.

She paused. That wall was real.

Surya dropped one of his leather carving tools. The sound landed twice.

The first? A clang.

The second? A wet thump.

He followed the clang.

Agni listened. A mantra whispered from the stone—his own voice from a childhood memory. He followed it and passed through a wall of light.

One by one, they found each other in a circular node at the center. The moment they joined hands, the next doorway lit.

They passed together.

Puzzle Three:

The next chamber was darker, filled with ropes and counterweights, pulleys strung across a tiled floor. In the center stood a dais with three levers, each guarded by a carved figure representing Brahma, Vishnu, and Shiva.

Above them, an inscription glowed:

"केवल वह खींच सकता है, जो स्वयं पर संदेह करता है। अन्यथा, भार असंतुलित होगा।"

"Only one who doubts may pull. Else the weight will break the balance."

Ropes on either side coiled toward pressure plates. If stepped on too heavily—or by the wrong person—the floor might collapse.

They stared at each other.

“I’ve carried purpose for too long,” Agni whispered. “I’m too committed.”

Hansika shook her head. “I’ve followed more than I’ve chosen.”

Surya looked down. “I’ve never believed I belonged here.”

He stepped forward and pulled the lever of Vishnu—the preserver, the balancer.

The ropes tightened—then relaxed.

Balance had been achieved.

The room shifted.

The final passage opened.

The last room was silent.

A single arch stood before them—carved with a celestial wheel.

Above it, three glowing runes floated:

- A flame
- A cracked coin
- A lotus blooming from ash

Below, a stone pedestal held a verse:

"सत्य वह नहीं जो बताया गया,

सत्य वह है जो तुमने अनुभव किया।

बाहर जाने के लिए पहचानो—

क्या अब तुम्हारे भीतर जीवित है?"

"Truth is not what was told, but what you've lived.

To leave, name what still lives in you."

Hansika studied the options.

"The flame… symbol of Agni's fire."

"The coin…" Surya said, "our choice."

"The lotus?" Agni asked. "A new beginning."

Just then, the room dimmed.

Raktadeva's voice seeped through the walls:

"What you've learned means nothing. The mountain will break you. The sky will burn you. Choose the flame… and I give you power. Choose the coin… and I let you rot. Choose wrong… and you'll never leave."

A gust of burning air swept through the chamber.

Hansika didn't flinch. "He wants fear."

Surya stepped forward. "Then we choose what he doesn't want."

Agni pressed the coin.

The arch glowed.

The door opened.

Raktadeva screamed—but could not follow.

They stepped through and emerged onto a high ledge, the sky stretched before them in hues of red and gold. Below- a sea of mist. In the distance, like a crown of heaven

Mount Sumeru.

Behind them, the Chamber of Echoes sealed with a soundless finality.

Agni opened his palm.

The spiral flame medallion burned bright, pulsing with the warmth of earned wisdom.

They had not survived by luck.

They had succeeded through unity, through ancient cunning, and through faith in the truth they carved together.

Ahead, the final ascent waited.

And none of them would face it alone.

***

Chapter Eight:
The Valley of Whispers

The descent from the Chamber of Echoes brought no peace—only a silence so deep it pressed against their lungs like stone. The terrain beyond was neither earth nor wilderness, but something in between—a valley hollowed out by forgotten grief. The ground was soft, like ashes beaten into soil, and the trees stood like mourners—gnarled, skeletal, and permanently bent as though in eternal lament. Their limbs reached out in silent despair, frozen mid-wail.

Mist rolled across the floor of the valley, thick and low, clinging not to the air but to memory. The moment Agni, Hansika, and Surya stepped foot onto the charred path, the whispers began.

At first, faint murmurs—barely the breeze.

Then clearer.

Voices.

Familiar. Foreign. Fractured.

But not spoken aloud. They *slid* beneath the skin, *wove* through thought.

Hansika slowed. Her eyes scanned the mist. "They're not illusions," she whispered. "They're... listening."

Agni's fire didn't light. His hands sparked, then died.

"There's no wind," he murmured, "but something is... breathing."

Surya froze. His shoulders stiffened. "I swear… I just heard my father laugh."

Then, without warning, the mist split—not physically, but psychically. Sound and sight desynchronized. Their eyes still saw each other—but their voices no longer matched mouths, and time stuttered like a broken chant.

It wasn't confusion.

It was invasion.

Their minds weren't just haunted—they were *inhabited.*

A single narrow stone path emerged—suspended just above the ground, bordered by moss-covered pale totems shaped like elongated faces. Each wept blood-red sap from closed eyes.

Some wore the faces of loved ones.

Others… wore theirs.

As they stepped forward, the whispers changed. They no longer murmured—they accused.

"You left her behind."

"He chose you because he was afraid."

"This fire is your vanity."

"He will betray you. She already doubts you."

And then the path shifted. The valley retaliated.

Each step grew heavier—not metaphorically, but physically.

Agni dropped to one knee as a satchel appeared across his back—stitched with burnt parchment and fused bone. Its weight was crushing. Flames smoldered at the seams, branding his shoulders with *doubt.*

Hansika gasped as iron chains coiled around her arms, forged from the echo of every judgment she had ever received—her mother's silences, the village's gossip, her own self-doubt.

Surya staggered as a wooden yoke snapped onto his back—two heavy buckets hanging from it, each filled with sandals he had mended for people who had never thanked him, never remembered his name.

Even the path beneath them changed—now shifting into cracked glass, then jagged thorns, then into a deep, shuddering stillness. Their breath became loud in their own heads. Their hearts pounded like drums in a vacuum.

And the whispers drilled deeper:

"She doesn't love you."

"You're not needed."

"This fire is a curse, not a gift."

"You are replaceable."

Surya collapsed.

"I can't move."

Hansika reached for him—but her chains tangled around her legs, dragging her down.

Agni gritted his teeth, clawing at the flaming satchel—but the fire licked at his skin and hissed, *"You're only burning them, not saving them."*

Then-

Hansika looked up.

Her breath shuddered. "We're not supposed to carry our own burdens."

She turned to Agni, looped her arm beneath his satchel, and **lifted with him**.

The flames **dimmed**.

Agni gasped, and with trembling hands, snapped the lock on Hansika's chain.

It shattered like glass.

Surya looked up through sweat and fog. Agni reached down and took one of his buckets.

The yoke loosened.

The moss hissed.

The totems turned their carved faces *away*.

And the path—cleared.

They reached the heart of the valley—a dried riverbed of slate and quartz. Along its cracked floor, stone mouths gaped open, as if frozen mid-chant.

At their feet, carved tiles spread in every direction, each etched with a phrase. Some glowed softly. Others cracked if touched.

An unseen voice murmured—deep, old:

"एक झूठ बोलता है।

एक संदेह करता है।

एक याद रखता है।

केवल सत्य के पथ पर चलो।

पर सत्य सबका नहीं होता।"

"One lies. One doubts. One remembers.

Walk only on the path of truth.

But truth does not belong to all."

It wasn't just a riddle—it was a team challenge.

Agni sensed deception, pointing out the tiles that pulsed with half-truths.

Hansika sensed energy, picking up subtle shifts of warmth from tiles that welcomed her presence.

Surya remembered the pattern, watching for repetition and mapping their steps.

Only when they surrendered to each other's insight, stepping beyond their own assumptions, did the correct path emerge.

Trust—not knowledge—carved their passage.

They crossed the riverbed, breathless but unbroken.

Beyond the mists, a crumbling temple stood like a mausoleum of memory—its roof cracked open to the dim sky, its stones held together more by devotion than mortar.

A plaque above the stone steps read:

"यहाँ वे हैं जो चले, पर याद नहीं रखे गए।

न प्रशंसा मिली, न प्रेम।

फिर भी चले। फिर भी गिरे।"

"Here lie those who walked the path but were never remembered.

Unpraised. Unloved.

Still—they walked."

Inside, at the heart of the open sanctum, a still pool of silver water reflected no one's face. Only stars.

And waiting beside it—The Older Man.

But he was no longer veiled.

His robes shimmered with threads of cosmic light. His face was both ancient and kind, and his presence silenced the valley.

"You did not resist the valley," he said softly. "You endured it by choosing each other."

Agni stepped forward. "Are we close?"

The Older Man nodded.

"You are no longer three travelers. You are now a single force."

Hansika stepped closer. "Who are you?"

The man smiled.

"Once—Dharmadeva. Guardian of the Pandavas' path. Now—I am but witness to those who dare walk it again."

Surya's voice cracked. "And Raktadeva?"

Dharmadeva turned his gaze to the east, toward the mountains cloaked in cloud.

"He awaits. His shrine is built not from stone…

But from the shattered promises of gods."

"He knows you come.

And he will not yield."

The silver pool shimmered—and showed them the truth.

Draupadi, weeping in snow.

Bhima, roaring before vanishing into mist.

Nakula and Sahadeva, arms outstretched, fading into silence.

And then—

Yudhishthira.

Barefoot. Alone. But whole.

"He bore the burden," Dharmadeva whispered. "So must you."

He stepped forward and laid his hand on Agni's shoulder.

The fire inside Agni settled—not extinguished, but clarified.

Like a torch no longer fed by fear, but by purpose.

Then—Dharmadeva faded.

Into light. Mist. Memory.

As they stepped outside, the mist no longer suffocated. Instead, golden fireflies danced like prayers.

The valley behind them whispered no longer in accusation—but in acknowledgment.

Agni tightened his grip on the obsidian blade—now warm against his back.

Hansika adjusted her scarf and looped it around her neck, brushing Surya's arm as she stepped beside him.

They didn't walk in a line anymore.

They walked side by side.

Toward the River of Remembrance.

Toward the final trial.

Where truth… would no longer just be a test.

But a cost.

***

Chapter Nine:
The Wrath Beneath the Mountain

The trail of fireflies led them into silence—so deep it pressed against the skin.

Where once the Shrine of Forgotten Names shimmered in memory, now only mist remained—a ghost released, a page turned. Agni, Hansika, and Surya pressed on, their feet silent on soft ash, guided by the Older Man's cryptic words:

"One more valley lies ahead...

Follow the fireflies.

Cross the River of Remembrance."

But as they turned the final bend through the starlit woods, the world opened—and shattered expectation.

There was no river.

No shimmer.

No reflection.

Only a wound in the world.

Before them lay a sunken crater, vast and cracked, its basin carved by ancient fire and fury. Black smoke curled upward like spirits denied release. The ground bled with heat—spiderwebs of magma glowed faintly red beneath ash-coated stone. The air pulsed—not with life, but with the echo of something vast, watching.

Hansika drew her scarf over her mouth. "What happened here?"

Agni knelt, hand grazing the scorched ground. "This isn't just destruction… it's punishment. Controlled. Designed."

A sudden gust of blistering wind howled from the crater.

It screamed like metal, and knocked them back.

The ash danced—and the earth split open with a roar that drowned out thought.

From the chasm rose a being so immense the world seemed to hold its breath.

Raktadeva.

Not merely a creature—but a fallen god incarnate. He towered above them, forged in molten obsidian, veins aglow with embered scripture. Wings of fire and ash unfurled from his back—each feather etched with forgotten curses. His eyes were not eyes, but dying suns. Bleeding, seething.

And when he spoke—mountains wept.

"You trespass on sacred ash.

You wear medallions not earned.

You walk where the Pandavas bled—

And so, you must burn."

Agni's fire instinctively blazed. The medallion on his chest pulsed.

But before he could react—

Raktadeva raised a finger.

A shockwave of divine force exploded outward—silent, colorless, unstoppable.

Hansika and Surya were thrown like leaves in a storm, their bodies slamming into boulders, trees, stone. The sky turned gray with dust. Hansika rolled twice before crashing into a pillar. Surya struck a cliff edge and crumpled to the ground.

Agni stumbled forward, shielding his face.

His flame—

extinguished mid-air.

Raktadeva descended slowly, his feet never touching earth. He hovered above the scorched crater like a final judgment.

"Fire belongs to the gods," he growled. "You are but a spark, Agni.

A spark begging to be seen."

Surya groaned, blood streaking his brow. His shoulder hung limp, dislocated. But he grit his teeth, stepped back, and slammed it into place with a sickening pop.

Then—he ran.

No hesitation.

He charged Raktadeva, hammer drawn.

The god didn't flinch.

Surya leapt—hammer striking Raktadeva's breastplate with thunder—

—but Raktadeva absorbed the impact, grinned, and unleashed a backhand that hurled Surya into a stone column. The cliff cracked on impact.

Hansika appeared behind the god, her body moving with wind-carved grace, twin daggers flashing.

She struck—

Her blade found a seam in his armor—slid in.

But before she could twist—

Raktadeva turned, faster than thought, and struck her with an open palm, sending her sailing through the air like a ragdoll. She hit the ground hard, ribs snapping.

Agni screamed.

And the world ignited.

His fire returned—not red, not orange, but white-hot and blinding, dancing up his arms, through his chest. The obsidian blade—still warm from Vaikara—glowed with Sanskrit runes that pulsed like a divine heartbeat.

He launched himself at Raktadeva, the blade trailing fire through the night.

Their blades met.

Metal shrieked.

Raktadeva roared. "You dare wield Vaikara's betrayal?!"

Agni struck again—then again—each slash empowered not by rage, but purpose. Fire wrapped around his body like armor, sparking sigils in the air with every move.

But Raktadeva's power was relentless.

With a snarl, he dodged and twisted, stepping inside Agni's swing—and drove his sword downward.

The obsidian blade cracked.

Then shattered.

Agni staggered.

His fire dimmed.

And Raktadeva punched him full in the chest—a molten fist powered by divine fury.

Agni's body exploded backward, crashing through the rock floor, buried beneath stone and silence.

Hansika screamed.

She crawled—her leg twisted, lips torn. "Agni—"

Surya rose again, limping, his hammer lost.

He charged barehanded.

He tackled Raktadeva mid-step—a mortal against a god.

"You don't get to break us!" he yelled.

He punched him—once, twice—blood streaming from his face.

Raktadeva didn't bleed.

But—he paused.

Something about that blow. That spirit.

That human defiance.

Beneath the rubble, Agni's body sparked.

His chest—where Raktadeva struck—began to glow. Not with pain.

But with marking.

A spiral flame burned across his heart—a divine brand. A seal.

Raktadeva raised his sword.

"To dust, then."

But the wind shifted.

And the mountains howled.

From the heavens above—silver fire descended.

The earth trembled.

A voice boomed—ancient, divine, irrefutable:

"You will not take them, Raktadeva.

Not yet."

From the smoke walked Dharmadeva—the Older Man no longer veiled, no longer hiding. His robes shimmered with scripture, and his staff burned with justice.

He struck the ground.

The earth split with holy fury.

Raktadeva reeled, hurled backward—roaring, smoking, his wings sputtering sparks.

"This path is not yours to guard," Dharmadeva said, voice echoing like a thousand bells.

"It belongs to those who walk it true."

Raktadeva hissed.

"You walk because I allow it," he growled. "And soon… I won't."

He vanished in a cyclone of smoke and ash.

Silence returned—thick, tense, shivering.

Hansika cradled Agni's body, weeping as blood soaked into his tunic.

But then—he stirred.

He gasped.

The flame on his chest pulsed, steady.

"I'm… still here," he whispered.

Surya staggered over, bruised, breathing hard.

Dharmadeva knelt, placed something beside Agni.

Not the blade.

But the hilt.

It glowed—alive.

"The weapon must now grow with you," Dharmadeva said. "Forged by your trials. Fed by your truth."

Agni nodded, barely.

Hansika pressed her forehead to his.

Surya closed his eyes, exhaling as stars returned overhead.

They looked up.

Beyond the crater, the peak of Mount Sumeru gleamed in the sky—closer than ever.

But above it—

The heavens burned red.

Not from fire.

From war.

***

Chapter Ten: Echoes of the Great War

The cold here was not of this world.

It didn't bite the skin.

It carved the soul.

The wind carried no sound, yet the silence was deafening—heavy, oppressive, ancient. Every footstep across the frozen basin echoed like a drumbeat in a forgotten tomb.

Above, the sun floated like an eye veiled in grief—its light dulled, not by clouds, but by time itself.

Agni stopped short.

His boot crunched on something solid beneath the snow.

Not ice.

Not stone.

Metal.

He brushed the frost aside.

Beneath lay a rusted helm, a broken spear, and a shattered war conch—its mouthpiece sealed with age. Twisted remnants of chariots jutted from the earth like bones. Around them, the ground bore ancient scorch marks and embedded arrows—a battlefield lost to memory.

Then Hansika gasped.

She knelt beside a bronze crown, half-buried in frost. Its edges were dulled, but the etching on its band still read:

"For dharma, for blood, for heaven."

Her voice trembled. "This is where they fell. The Pandavas… their final stand."

But the scriptures had said nothing of this.

The scrolls ended at Mount Sumeru.

There had been no mention of a war beyond heaven's path.

And yet—here it was.

A graveyard sealed by silence.

Suddenly, the wind stopped.

Not died—paused.

The air thickened.

And from the mountains above, whispers fell—not sounds, but memories. The ground trembled as if exhaling its long-held breath.

And then—reality split.

Before their eyes, the snow turned to ash. The battlefield bloomed anew—not a vision, but a resurrection of history. Flames rose. Smoke billowed.

Drums pounded like heartbeats of the dead.

And standing in the midst of it all—

The Pandavas.

Young. Bloodied.

But unbroken.

Yudhishthira stood with staff in hand, his eyes sorrowful.

Bhima, dented mace dragging beside him.

Arjuna loosed arrows that shimmered like lightning.

Nakula and Sahadeva fought back-to-back, blades dancing with divine precision.

Agni whispered, "We're not dreaming… this is the war that was erased."

Hansika nodded, stunned. "The war that followed the journey. The one no one was meant to remember."

Then—the sky tore open.

A fireball plummeted from the heavens, trailing black smoke and shattered mantras.

When it struck the earth, the ground convulsed.

Raktadeva rose.

Cloaked in flame, armored in broken celestial sigils, crowned with shadow. His wings of scorched scripture spread wide, blocking out the sun. His presence was not a thing to be seen—but endured.

"They thought they had won," he roared, his voice splitting stone.

"But dharma was never theirs to claim.

And neither shall it be yours."

He turned toward Agni and the others.

"You are the embers of their ambition.

And I shall extinguish you."

He slammed his fist into the ground.

It shattered.

From the cracks emerged an army of the forsaken:

- Skeletons in burnt armor.
- Cursed chariots pulled by beasts made of ash.
- Specters of the Kauravas—led by Dushasana's glowing red eyes.
- Demons with jaws unhinged, tongues flicking fire.

The sky turned blood red.

Surya stepped forward, hammer in hand, bruised but unbowed.

"We've never faced anything like this," he said.

Agni clenched his fists. "But we've changed."

Hansika's eyes gleamed. "Then we finish what they started."

And the war ignited.

Agni blazed forward—no longer just fire, but wrath wrapped in prayer. The broken hilt in his hand grew into a new blade—one forged from his will. He tore through shadows, divine fire flaring with each strike.

Hansika moved like stormlight—daggers flashing, eyes fierce, slicing through specters with a dancer's grace.

Surya was an unstoppable wall—blocking, bashing, protecting, enduring everything the world threw at them.

But then—Raktadeva descended.

He landed with a blast that split the earth.

Hansika was hurled toward a canyon. She clawed at the edge, her fingers bleeding.

Agni reached for her. "Give me your hand!"

But—

Raktadeva appeared behind him, blade raised.

And struck.

Surya dove—took the blow.

The blade pierced his side with brutal force.

He collapsed against a broken altar, blood spilling into snow.

"Hansika… Agni…" he gasped.

Hansika screamed.

Rage and grief twisted her features—but Agni didn't cry out.

He rose.

Something within him broke open.

Not rage.

Not revenge.

But clarity.

Golden mantras blazed across his arms, legs, chest.

His spine straightened.

His flame became formless.

He floated upward, surrounded by radiant Sanskrit symbols.

His voice echoed like the scriptures reborn.

"You were once a guardian, Raktadeva.

But you fell.

Not because you failed the gods—

But because you forgot compassion."

He extended his blade—not of steel now, but divine light.

"We did not come to conquer heaven.

We came to understand it."

And he hurled the blade.

It spun through the air like judgment.

Raktadeva raised his sword to block—

But the divine fire struck his chest.

The runes on Agni's blade blazed brighter than the sun.

They didn't pierce.

They unmade.

Raktadeva screamed—not in pain, but in release.

His form cracked.

His wings shattered.

And slowly—he disintegrated, like a curse finally broken.

Ash fell like snow.

Silence returned.

Hansika held Surya, sobbing.

He coughed, eyes fluttering.

"Did… we make it?"

She nodded, smiling through tears. "You saved us."

Agni knelt beside them, the light fading from his eyes.

He wasn't a boy anymore.

He wasn't fire.

He was something more.

From the far ridge, the mist parted.

A staircase emerged—woven from light, smoke, and truth.

The Gates of Heaven had returned.

And from the edge—

The Older Man appeared.

His hood was gone.

His eyes were eternal.

He looked at them—each of them—and spoke with sorrow and pride:

"You have passed through fire, through doubt, through wrath.

But now…

One may step forward.

One may ascend."

The wind stilled.

The mountain listened.

And the question remained—

Who will it be?

***

Chapter Eleven:
The Final Revelation

The battlefield behind them was quiet now—blanketed in ash and the soft, flickering remnants of fire. Victory had not come in cheers, but in survival.

Surya limped slightly, blood dried around the torn fabric of his tunic. Hansika's hands still trembled, not from fear—but from everything she had seen, endured, chosen.

Agni stood silent, the heat at his core no longer blazing—but steady. His fire had become something more than flame. It had become purpose.

And ahead—rising from the mist like a memory returning—was the staircase.

It shimmered like a mirage: each step woven not from stone, but from light, breath, and memory. It floated in the air, suspended by nothing—yet it pulsed with the weight of eons.

Agni stepped closer. His legs trembled—not from fatigue, but from the weight of what this meant.

Hansika tightened her grip on Surya's side and whispered, "We're here. We made it."

But Agni did not respond. His gaze locked onto the path ahead, and something deep inside him whispered:

Not yet.

Then—the wind changed.

Clouds parted. The world held its breath.

From the ridge above, a figure descended. Slowly. Silently.

The Older Man.

But now, he was no longer a shadow in robes. His steps echoed like distant temple bells. His garments shimmered—threads of **starlight and sacred ink**, as though he had been written into existence.

Agni turned. "Who are you?"

Hansika stepped forward. "Why did you follow us?"

The man smiled—eyes heavy with centuries, yet clear.

"Because I walked this path long before you.

And I will walk it long after.

I am the test. The truth. The final answer."

Then his form shimmered:

- A lion—fierce and royal.
- A bull—unmoving, unshakable.
- An elephant—wise and solemn.
- A radiant sage, glowing with divinity.

And then—just a man again. The Older Man.

Hansika gasped.

Even Surya stirred.

Agni's breath caught.

"He's not… human. He's—Dharma."

The man nodded.

"And I am your father, Agni."

The words echoed in the cold air.

Agni staggered.

"My father? But… my parents—they died. I never knew them."

Dharma's voice was gentle. Eternal.

"They lived—but not in the way you understand.

You are the son of a promise, not of flesh.

Born from a fire that seeks truth.

You are the last ember of those who dared and failed… and still hoped."

Hansika reached for Agni's arm, steadying him.

Dharma's gaze fell upon all three of them.

"Agni was never meant to reach heaven.

He was meant to awaken the truth:

That heaven is not for the proud, or the obsessed.

It is for the selfless.

He was meant to learn. To burn.

And most of all—to choose."

He turned and raised his hand to the staircase.

"One may ascend.

Only one.

The soul must go forward—unburdened.

Alone."

Agni's chest tightened.

Hansika's breath hitched.

Surya groaned softly. "Don't leave me behind…"

Hansika whispered, her voice shaking, "This was always your path, Agni."

But Agni stepped back.

"No. It wasn't mine alone.

I would've never made it without you.

You both believed in me—when I didn't even believe in myself."

He looked up at Dharma.

"Is there no other way?"

Dharma's eyes shimmered—not with power, but with understanding.

"Even gods must choose."

Agni walked to the first stair.

The light touched him—welcoming. It called to something deep inside.

He stood there—one foot on eternity.

Then he thought of:

—Surya, throwing himself into death's path.

—Hansika, crying out, shielding him, believing.

—Everything they had lost, everything they had become.

He stepped back.

And turned to them both.

"You two… are my heaven.

I don't need to go anywhere else."

Hansika's knees gave. She sobbed.

Surya looked away—but his hand found Agni's shoulder.

Dharma's eyes glistened.

"Then… you have passed."

The staircase began to dissolve.

But it did not vanish.

It changed—its light softening into golden mist, flowing like breath.

The path ahead was no longer above them.

It stretched forward—earthbound, eternal.

Dharma stepped closer.

He placed a hand on Agni's head.

"You chose well.

The heavens are not a destination.

They are a reflection of the soul."

He turned to Hansika.

"You loved selflessly.

You carried Draupadi's grace—but not her pain."

To Surya:

"Your pride nearly ruined you.

But your loyalty, your willingness to bleed for love—saved you."

He raised his hand.

Surya's wounds faded.

Only scars remained.

And they no longer hurt.

They stood together—at the edge of the world.

Before them, Mount Sumeru blazed against a sky of silver flame and purple wind.

Mantras floated on the breeze.

The universe breathed with them.

Dharma's voice was quieter now.

"Your story does not end here.

The world needs your fire.

Your truth.

Your light."

He began to fade.

"Go. Walk forward.

And let others learn from your journey.

For true heaven…

is the path walked with a pure heart."

Then—he was gone.

They stood in silence.

Then…

Agni turned.

Hansika took Surya's hand.

And they walked—not toward the gates of heaven.

But into the world.

Changed.

Wiser.

Together.

And far above, hidden in the clouds beyond Mount Sumeru…

five warriors watched—

cloaked in golden dust,

their eyes alight with pride.

And they smiled.

***

Epilogue: The Soulless One Watches

The forest exhaled around them, quiet and alive.

No birds announced their return. No petals fell in welcome. And yet, the stillness felt right—like the earth itself had paused to acknowledge what they had survived.

Agni, Hansika, and Surya stepped out of the mist just as the village stirred with first light. Their silhouettes were changed—etched with fire and shadow, as if the journey had carved truths into their bones.

They said nothing as they walked the familiar path home. Not because they had nothing to say—

But because words would never carry what they had become.

When they crossed the last field, the village did not notice.

But two people did.

Surya's grandmother stood in the doorway, arms folded, lips tight.

"Where have you been?" she snapped, storming toward him. "Fourteen days! Fourteen! I nearly went to the priests! I thought you were buried under a banyan root or run off to Varanasi to sell sandals to monks!"

Surya winced as she gripped his arm—but he didn't speak.

He couldn't explain.

Instead, he quietly stepped inside, placed his pack by the wall…
and gently kissed her wrinkled forehead.
She blinked.
The boy who had left was gone.
This one… was something else.
He still hammered soles by day—but now, the blows were quieter, steadier. Not chasing pride, but building peace.
And when he spoke to customers, they listened.
Not because his words were louder.
But because his silence had learned to speak.

Hansika's mother was waiting too—veil wrapped tight, worry storming in her eyes.
"You vanished. Not even a note. What am I to tell the neighbors? That my daughter wandered off alone somewhere without telling her mother?"

Hansika hugged her without a word.
For a moment, her mother stiffened… then softened.
There was something in Hansika's eyes now—steel beneath sunlight.

She moved with grace, but no longer sought approval. She walked like someone who had survived the wind and chosen where to plant her feet.

Later that evening, Hansika returned to the riverbank—where reeds swayed in rhythm with her breath. She watched her reflection.

And it didn't matter what she saw.

Because now… she knew who she was even when the water blurred.

As for Agni. No one waited for him.

No door creaked open. No name was called.

But he didn't need it.

He returned to the banyan tree at the village's edge—the same tree where his search had begun, where whispers of heaven had first stirred in his heart.

He sat beneath its roots, spine straight, hands open.

He did not pray.

He listened.

To the way the leaves rustled like old verses.

To the hum of earth, as if remembering him.

To the pulse of a world he had stopped trying to escape—and had begun to understand.

He no longer burned to reach the heavens.

Now, he burned to make the ground sacred.

They never spoke of the journey—not to anyone.

Not because they were ashamed.

But because the truth didn't belong in words anymore.

It lived in who they had become.

And still… something watched.

Far beyond Mount Sumeru, beyond mortal knowing and divine sight.

In a place untouched by fire or time—

Nirātmā stirred.

The Soulless One.

Where Raktadeva had burned in fury, Nirātmā floated in absence.

No hunger.

No rage.

No heartbeat.

Just… nothing.

The kind of nothing that swallowed stars whole.

He did not speak.

He did not breathe.

He did not judge.

But he watched.

And when Agni opened his eyes beneath the banyan tree, a chill traced the back of his neck.

It was not the wind.

It was attention.

Something ancient. Nameless.

As if a void in the sky had blinked.

As if the universe had noticed him back.

The path was not over.

It had only just begun.

And somewhere in the dark…

the Soulless One waited.

***

TEASER FOR BOOK 2

Book Two: The Shadows Beneath the Light

The Shadows Beneath the Light — *Coming Soon*

They reached the Gates of Heaven.
They returned changed.
But some doors, once opened, echo far beyond their threshold.

In the stillness of their village, the wind carries voices no one remembers speaking.
Reflections linger too long. Dreams dissolve into silence.
And a child with wordless eyes watches it all.

Agni's fire falters.
Hansika hears truths no one else can.
Surya feels strength slipping into something stranger.

They thought the path had ended.
But darkness does not always follow behind.
Sometimes… it waits ahead.

A Note to the Reader

Dear Reader,

Thank you for walking this path with me.
If this story touched your heart, stirred your spirit, or lit even a spark within you—I'd be honored to hear your thoughts.

Please consider leaving a review—it helps stories like this find more readers.
Share it with someone who might need a little fire in their soul.

And if you'd like to follow the journey toward Book Two, connect with me on Instagram.

Your time, your attention, your belief—it means everything.
Keep walking. Keep burning bright.

With love,
Simran Pal

Stay Connected

Thank you for joining Agni, Hansika, and Surya on their journey through fire, truth, and the unknown.

This is only the beginning.

If the story touched your heart, made you think, or even made you laugh or cry—I'd love to hear from you.

Let's keep in touch:

Email: simranpal907@gmail.com

Instagram: @simranpal.907

Get bonus lore & a free prequel PDF: *Coming soon!*

Merch, bookmarks, and more: *Stay tuned on Instagram!*

Your reviews, messages, shares, and support help independent authors like me grow, create, and continue to tell stories.

From the gates of heaven to the heart of a reader—thank you for walking this path with us.

See you in the next book.

With warmth and stardust,
Simran Pal Kaur
Author of *Journey to the Gates of Heaven*

www.ingramcontent.com/pod-product-compliance
Lightning Source LLC
Chambersburg PA
CBHW050020170726
48282CB00025B/481
9789334376289